For Hector and for the volunteers —P. B.

For my uncles Rene, Pete, John B., and
Edward "Lalo" Parra for their good humor,
old stories, and great family memories. —J. P.

Text copyright © 2015 by Phil Bildner.
Illustrations copyright © 2015 by John Parra.
All rights reserved. No part of this book may be reproduced in
any form without written permission from the publisher.

Library of Congress Cataloging-in-Publication Data:

Bildner, Phil.
  Marvelous Cornelius : Hurricane Katrina and the spirit of New
Orleans / by Phil Bildner ; illustrations by John Parra.
    pages cm
  Summary: A man sings and dances his way through the French
Quarter in New Orleans, keeping his beloved city clean, until
Hurricane Katrina's devastation nearly causes him to lose his
spirit.
  ISBN 978-1-4521-2578-7 (alk. paper)
[1. Refuse collectors—Fiction. 2. Hurricane Katrina, 2005—Fic-
tion. 3. African Americans—Fiction. 4. New Orleans (La.)—Fic-
tion.] I. Title.

PZ7.B4923Mar 2015
[E]—dc23

  2013043742

Manufactured in China.

MIX
Paper from
responsible sources
FSC™ C104723

Design by Ryan Hayes.
Typeset in Farao.
The illustrations in this book were rendered in paint.

10 9 8 7

Chronicle Books LLC
680 Second Street
San Francisco, California 94107

Chronicle Books—we see things differently. Become part of our
community at www.chroniclekids.com.

MARVELOUS CORNELIUS

Hurricane Katrina and the Spirit of New Orleans

By **Phil Bildner**

Illustrated by **John Parra**

chronicle books · san francisco

Even if it's called your lot to be a street sweeper, go out and sweep streets like Michelangelo painted pictures, sweep streets like Handel and Beethoven composed music, sweep streets like Shakespeare wrote poetry. Sweep streets so well that all the hosts of heaven and earth will have to pause and say, "Here lived a great street sweeper who swept his job well."

—Martin Luther King Jr.

In the Quarter,
there worked a man
known in New Orleans as Marvelous Cornelius.

"Mornin'." He saluted the silver-haired man with the *Times-Picayune* tucked under his arm.

"Greetings." He waved to the couple
with the baby on the balcony.
"Ma'am." He nodded to the woman
shaking rugs out at her front window.

And when his truck rounded the turn . . .

"My young'uns!" he called to the kids crowding the corner.

"Marvelous Cornelius!" they cheered. "Marvelous Cornelius!"

At each home, Cornelius sashayed to the curb and shimmied to the hopper.
Unloading the garbage, not a single praline wrapper ever stayed on the streets.
And those spotless streets, oh, how they sparkled.

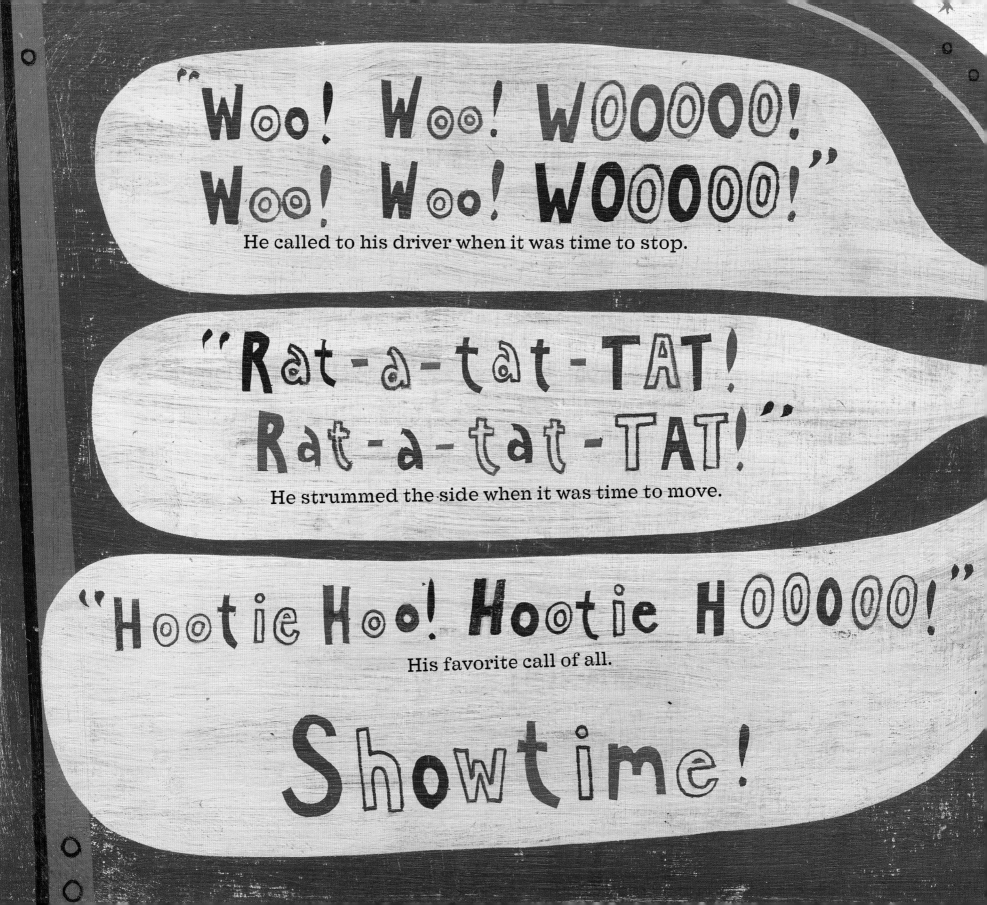

"Woo! Woo! WOOOOO! Woo! Woo! WOOOOO!"

He called to his driver when it was time to stop.

"Rat-a-tat-TAT! Rat-a-tat-TAT!"

He strummed the side when it was time to move.

"Hootie Hoo! Hootie HOOOOO!"

His favorite call of all.

Showtime!

Cornelius front flipped to the curb
and flung the bags over his head
behind his back
between his legs
into the truck.

He lined bags along the curb and then launched them.
Bag after bag after bag after bag after bag.
They landed in a perfect pyramid inside the hopper's metal mouth.

BANG!

He clapped the covers like cymbals and
twirled the tins like tops. Whizzing and
spinning back and forth across the street.

And just like those twisting tops, Cornelius danced, too.

Tango-ing up Toulouse.

Samba-ing down St. Peter.

Rumba-ing up Royal.

Cha-cha-ing down Chartres.

And everyone danced along.

The old ladies whistled and whirled.
The old men hooted and hollered.
The barbers, bead twirlers, and
beignet bakers bounded behind
the one-man parade.

But then one day, the storm came.
The great city filled with water.

People and pets, parks and playgrounds, washed away.
Schools and shops, streets and streetcars, washed away.

For far too long
water, water, everywhere.
A gumbo of mush and mud.

When those waters finally fell away, Cornelius
looked out at the mountains of ruins—some as
high as the steeple atop St. Louis Cathedral.

"It would take thousands of me to clean this."

He wept. "Millions."

Cornelius rose.
He dried his eyes.
For his spirit and will were
waterproof.

And just like he did every morning,
he emptied the garbage into his hopper.

And the kids who crowded the corner,
they pitched in, too.

So did the silver-haired man.
The couple from the balcony.
The woman with the rugs.
The old ladies and old men.
The barbers, bead twirlers,
and beignet bakers.

Others, too.
From Brooklyn and Boise, Baltimore
and Bakersfield. Syracuse, Seattle,
Santa Fe, San Antonio.

They streamed to the Crescent City.

Thousands.

Millions.

A flood of humanity.

"Hootie Hoo!"

Marvelous Cornelius cheered.

"Hootie HOOOOO!"

As the great city rose again,
Marvelous Cornelius,
he passed on.
But as for his spirit,
that's part of New Orleans,
New Orleans forever after.

AUTHOR'S NOTE

In the years following Hurricane Katrina, I visited New Orleans many times to help in the cleanup and recovery. Often, I chaperoned groups of teen volunteers. When I did, those trips always evolved into incredibly uplifting and life-affirming experiences.

They always became about the people.

One person I met was Katy Reckdahl, a reporter for the *Times-Picayune*. While Katrina was lashing the Gulf Coast in August of 2005, Katy was giving birth to her son, Hector, at Touro Infirmary in New Orleans's Garden District.

After meeting Katy, I read some of her archived articles, including one titled, "Talking Trash." It was a feature about Cornelius Washington, a sanitation worker in the French Quarter who sang, danced, and performed tricks—"a wizard of trash cans."

I had to learn about him.

Sadly, Cornelius passed away not long after Hurricane Katrina. But with Katy's help, I located his mother, Ms. Mary Wiley. Ms. Mary still lived in the tiny town of Waterproof, Louisiana, where she'd raised Cornelius.

Ms. Mary and I spoke on the phone several times. She sent me a letter, too, a handwritten letter filled with memories of Cornelius. Whenever I read it, it was as if the Cornelius I'd seen in video clips—the baldheaded man with the big hoop earring and the New Orleans drawl—was reading to me.

Cornelius's story has the flavor of folktales and folk heroes like John Henry, and by incorporating repetition, alliteration, and exaggeration, I have tried to honor those qualities in the telling. Still, it must be said that while Cornelius was certainly a showman, he may not have twirled lids like tops or clapped them like cymbals. He had signals and calls, but they weren't the exact ones described here. The garbage bags he threw into his hopper probably didn't land in perfect pyramids. Nor did the destruction following Katrina rise as high as the steeple atop St. Louis Cathedral. And though he was celebrated and beloved in his neighborhoods, he was not called Marvelous Cornelius.

But he deserves to be.

On so many levels, Cornelius symbolizes what the city of New Orleans is all about—the energy, the spirit, the magic, the people. That's what brought all those volunteers to the Crescent City, and inside each one was a little bit of Marvelous Cornelius.

◉ ◉ ◉

To find out more about the real Cornelius Washington and to learn how to write your own story in the American folk tradition, visit www.chroniclebooks.com/CorneliusWashington.

PRONUNCIATION GUIDE

Beignet—BEN-yay

Chartres—CHAR-ters

New Orleans—New OAR-linz

Praline—PRAW-leen

Royal—RERL (as in pearl)

Toulouse—TOO-loose